BECOME AN EXPER
WITH TRU

This three-level reading series is design
beginning readers or improving readers and is based on
True and the Rainbow Kingdom episodes. The books feature
common sight words used with limited grammar. Each book
also offers a set number of target words. These words are noted
in bold print and are presented in a picture dictionary in order
to reinforce meaning and expand reading vocabulary.

LEVEL
1
LITTLE STAR

For pre-readers to read along
- 125-175 words
- Simple sentences
- Simple vocabulary and common sight words
- Picture dictionary teaching 6 target words

LEVEL
2
RISING STAR

For beginning readers to read with support
- 175-250 words
- Longer sentences
- Limited vocabulary and more sight words
- Picture dictionary teaching 8 target words

LEVEL
3
SUPER STAR

For improving readers to read on their own or with support
- 250-350 words
- Longer sentences and more complex grammar
- Varied vocabulary and less-common sight words
- Picture dictionary teaching 10 target words

CrackBoom! Books is an imprint of Chouette Publishing (1987) Inc.

Text: adaptation by Robin Bright of the animated series TRUE AND THE RAINBOW KINGDOM™/MC, produced by Guru Studio.
Original script written by Doug Sinclair
Original episode #111: A Royal Stink
All rights reserved.

Illustrations: © GURU STUDIO. All Rights Reserved.

Chouette Publishing would like to thank the Government of Canada and SODEC for their financial support.

Books
Tax Credit

Gestion
SODEC

Bibliothèque et Archives nationales du Québec and Library and Archives Canada cataloguing in publication

Title: A royal stink / Robin Bright; illustrations, Guru Animation Studio.
Names: Bright, Robin, 1966- author. | Guru Studio (Firm), illustrator.
Description: Series statement: True and the rainbow kingdom | Read with True. Level 1 (little star)
Identifiers: Canadiana 2020008481X | ISBN 9782898022685 (softcover)
Classification: LCC PZ7.1.B75 Ro 2020 | DDC j813/.6—dc23

Legal deposit – Bibliothèque et Archives nationales du Québec, 2020.
Legal deposit – Library and Archives Canada, 2020.

Printed in Scott, Canada
10 9 8 7 6 5 4 3 2 1 CHO2105 JUL2020

MIX
Paper from
responsible sources
FSC® C103304

READ WITH

TRUE
and the RAINBOW KINGDOM

LEVEL
1
LITTLE STAR

A ROYAL STINK

Adaptation from the animated series: Robin Bright
Illustrations: © GURU STUDIO. All Rights Reserved.

CRACKBOOM!

The Rainbow **King**
has an idea.

He makes True a **queen**, just for today!

But there is a
bad smell in
True's kingdom.

The smell is from Mila's new
pet, Stinko! How can True
make the bad smell go away?

To the Wishing Tree!

Zee can smell the bad smell.
"Let's sit and have a think,"
he says.

"Wishing Tree,
please share your wonderful
Wishes with me!"

What are True's three Wishes?

Her first Wish can **spray** a good smell.

Her second Wish can suck air in and **blow** it out.

Her third Wish can make things smaller.

Thank you, Wishing Tree!

Mila and her pet are **sad**.
No one will play with Stinko
because he smells bad.

Time for True's first Wish!

The Wish **sprays** Stinko.

Stinko smells good!

But not for long.

True's second Wish sucks in the bad smell.

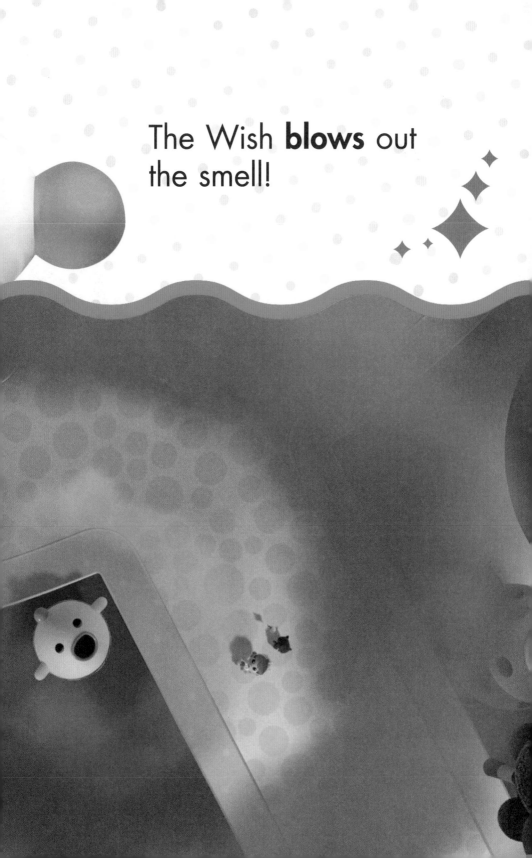

The Wish **blows** out
the smell!

"I need you!" says True to her third Wish.

True's last Wish
shrinks the **stink** cloud.
No more bad smell!

"True, you did it!" says the **King**.

Picture Dictionary

king

queen

sad

stink

blow

spray